W9-CIR-711

The Shadow ®

adapted by Les Martin
from the screenplay by David Koepp

BULLSEYE BOOKS

Random House 🏠 New York

Chapter 1

The black car roared down a dirt road on an errand of death.

It was sometime in the 1920s, in a faraway land called Tibet.

Tibet was then a small country squeezed between China and India. It was a wild land of snowcapped mountains and plunging valleys, dense forests and waving fields of flowers.

The car wound its way through a field thick with poppies. Workers harvested them. But they weren't after the beautiful flowers. They were interested only in the hard seeds. These seeds could be turned into opium. And that vile drug could be sold to its victims for gold. In Tibet, poppies had become flowers of evil.

Past the poppies, the car followed the road up a hill. Perched above the harvest stood a dark palace. The car stopped in front of it. The Tibetan driver got out and opened the passenger's door. He yanked out the passenger. When the passenger struggled, the driver pulled out a long knife. He held the cold blade to the passenger's throat. The passenger gave in. Together they entered the palace.

The passenger in the car was named Li Peng. He was strong and brave. But his strength did him no good as palace guards surrounded him. He trembled in fear of the man they were taking him to see.

That terrifying man ruled the palace. He ruled the poppy fields below. And the fields beyond them. Step by brutal step, he was taking over every poppy field in Tibet.

By now all Tibet whispered his name in dread. Ying Ko.

But all knew that this was not his real name. He was not a Tibetan. He was a Westerner, an American. But no one knew the name he went by in that distant land.

Now Li Peng was being brought to this man of mystery and menace. Li Peng wondered if he would live to tell the world what Ying Ko actually looked like.

Li Peng's eyes opened wide as he was led

through double doors into the vast throne room.

Hidden in shadow on his throne sat Ying Ko, dressed in clothes as black as night. Beside him stood his right-hand man, Wu. Protecting the ruler were huge guards. Idling like pampered pets around the room were hangers-on to amuse him.

Ying Ko said nothing when Li Peng was dragged before him. His assistant Wu did the talking.

"What do you have to say for yourself, Li Peng?" Wu demanded.

Still straining for a better look at Wu's master, Li Peng started to plead his case. "Listen to me. Try to be fair. Ying Ko asks too much. He does not need my poppy fields. They are a glass of water in a rainstorm compared to his."

Wu answered coldly, "Your brothers murdered three of our men."

Li Peng felt blind anger rise. "Ying Ko would have done the same. Send three more and I'll kill them, too."

Silence greeted his threat. He felt chilled. He tried to use reason instead of rage. "Ying Ko already controls so much land, and all of the opium trade. I'm entitled to my share."

Still more silence.

Li Peng played his last card. He spoke straight

to Ying Ko. "If you kill me, I promise that my brothers will come for *you*."

At last Li Peng got what he was looking for. A good look at Ying Ko.

Ying Ko leaned forward out of the shadow. For an instant Li Peng saw a harsh but handsome American face. Then all Li Peng saw were Ying Ko's eyes. Eyes as deep as endless space. Eyes that seemed to suck Li Peng's soul out of his body.

Li Peng heard Ying Ko's words, "I promise *you* that I'll bury your brothers beside you."

Ying Ko gave a casual wave of his hand. A guard put a dagger at Li Peng's throat.

Wu nodded at his master's decision. He started to walk out of the room. He worked with pen and ink rather than blades and blood.

As Wu passed by Li Peng, the desperate prisoner saw his chance. He slammed his heel down on the foot of the guard behind him. Whirling, he tore the dagger from a man's hand. Without pausing, he grabbed Wu. Now the dagger was at Wu's throat.

"I only wish to leave. Let me go!" Li Peng screamed at Ying Ko. "Wu is your friend, your right hand. Even you wouldn't take a chance of killing him." Li Peng paused to glare at the guards who had drawn their guns. Then he shouted, "Let me go! Your men aren't good enough shots to shoot around him."

Ying Ko grimaced. "You're right."

To Wu he said, "You've been a wonderful friend."

Then he nodded at the guards.

Ying Ko did not blink a dark eye as bullets ripped through Wu to kill Li Peng. Still unblinking, he watched his guards drag the two corpses away.

Then he yawned. It had been a long day. He would sleep well that night.

He was wrong. That night Ying Ko's sleep was disturbed by a dream. Or rather, Lamont Cranston's sleep was. For in slumberland, he was still Lamont Cranston, always Lamont Cranston.

He couldn't escape that name, no matter how far he fled. He couldn't destroy that name, no matter what he did. It was like a wound that wouldn't heal within him. And in his dreams the bandages came off.

In his dream tonight, Lamont Cranston encountered what he'd never believed existed.

For the first time Lamont Cranston met his master.

Chapter 2

Lamont Cranston woke with a start. His room was dark. It was the middle of the night.

The dream was still vivid in his mind. In it, he saw a face. The face was young, that of a boy no more than fifteen years old. Yet there was something very old about it. Ancient wisdom shone from its eyes like an eternal sun. Those eyes seemed to look into Lamont Cranston's secret heart. The heart that he kept hidden from the world. The heart that he hid even from himself.

Lamont Cranston tossed and turned in his sleep. He tried to escape the gaze of the young man, but he could not. When he woke, his body was covered with sweat. The sweat of his tortured night. And the sweat of a fear he could not name.

Then he heard the faintest of sounds. In the darkness he saw dim shadows on his balcony. The shadows glided swiftly into the room.

Cranston wiped the dream from his mind. He had more pressing things to worry about. At least he knew how to deal with *this* kind of threat. He grabbed a pistol from his night table. He leapt out of bed.

"Who's there?" he demanded, on his way to the light switch.

No one answered. Cranston flicked on the light.

Too late he saw a huge fist clubbing the gun from his hand. The next thing he knew, the fist smashed him in the face.

Lying on his back, Cranston saw stars. But in a moment, his vision cleared. Two enormous Tibetans were looking down at him.

"Who are you?" Cranston snarled.

Again there was no answer. One of the men merely clicked his tongue. The second bent down, lifted Cranston up, and slammed him down again.

Something snapped inside Cranston. His fists moved like triphammers. One-two, he bashed the second Tibetan in the stomach. The mountain-sized man doubled over. Cranston brought up a knee to smash the man's face. Then he whirled to take on the other one.

The first Tibetan launched a powerhouse

punch. Cranston ducked it easily. The force of the swing sent the Tibetan hurtling past him. Cranston smashed him on the back. Then Cranston jumped him. His hands went around the man's throat, squeezing as hard as he could...

A moment more, Cranston would have finished him off. But he didn't get that moment.

Something hit the back of his head like a sledgehammer.

That was the last thing he remembered until he felt himself being bounced up and down.

He opened his eyes. It was day. He was lying tied up hand and foot in the back of an oxcart. The oxcart was climbing a mountain road. The first Tibetan held the reins of the ox. The second stood guard over Cranston.

"You're Li Peng's brothers?" Cranston asked. His mind was racing. He was figuring out angles, hunting a way out of this death trap.

The Tibetan shook his head. His pitying look made it clear how wrong Cranston was.

"Then who are you? Where are you taking me?" Cranston said desperately. He wasn't used to being in the dark.

"A Tulku wishes to see you," the Tibetan said.

Cranston blinked in surprise. Then he grinned.

"A holy man wants to see *me*?" he said. "I can hardly wait. I can use a good laugh."

But the sight of their destination wiped the smile off Cranston's face.

The oxcart stopped at the base of a sheer mountain wall. A magnificent temple was built into the rock. Guarding the entrance was a carving of a gigantic cobra.

Cranston's jaw dropped. "I know this whole area. This was never here before."

The first Tibetan smiled. "The clouded mind sees nothing."

Cranston's feet were untied. He did not think of making a run for it. Through the entranceway he caught a glimpse of gold. He smelled loot. He would see what there was in there. Then he would figure out how to grab it.

He followed the Tibetans into the temple. Gold gilded the passageway. His mouth watered.

At the end of the passageway stood splendid doors. The Tibetans untied his hands. They motioned that Cranston should go on alone.

He did, eagerly. The gold in the passageway was like an appetizer. There had to be a feast of wealth beyond those doors.

The doors swung inward before Cranston

reached them, and he saw that he was right.

He entered a room ablaze with gold. Gold was everywhere. On the floors. The walls. The ceiling.

But suddenly Cranston stopped staring at it.

All he saw was the figure who sat on the throne at the end of the room.

The Tulku.

His shaven head gleamed in the bright torch-light reflecting off the gold.

His eyes gleamed with timeless wisdom.

His face was the boy's face in Cranston's dream.

Cranston tried to find his voice. "Who are you?" he croaked.

"You recognize me," the Tulku said, his voice gentle as ripples on water.

"No," Cranston said loudly. He felt afraid to admit the truth even to himself.

"You have seen me, as a picture in your mind," the Tulku said. "I am your teacher."

"Teacher, my foot," Cranston blustered. "I don't take lessons—I give orders. Do you have any idea who you just kidnapped?"

Smiling, the Tulku said, "Cranston. Lamont Cranston."

"You know my real name?" Cranston burst

out. His voice turned menacing. "You dare speak it?"

"Yes," the Tulku said, undisturbed. "And I know more. I know how long you've struggled against the evil within you. I know you've always lost. You've watched your spirit, your very face change, when the beast claws out from inside you. You are in great pain. Aren't you?"

That was all that Cranston needed to hear. Rage flooded through him once again.

"Pain? I'll show you what pain is," he snarled, and charged the boy.

"Wha—?" Cranston grunted. He lurched off-balance. The boy had vanished.

The Tulku's voice sounded through the room. "Lamont Cranston, you know what evil lurks in the hearts of men. You've seen that evil in your own. That makes you a powerful man. I intend to give you even more power. But a different power. For a different purpose."

Cranston turned in circles, looking for the boy. But there was only the Tulku's calm voice. "It may take a year, even more, to teach you to use your black shadow to *fight* evil. But it is the price you must pay to be saved."

Blinking, Cranston saw the boy suddenly appear a few feet away. Cranston saw red. "I'm not looking to be saved," Cranston snarled.

Cranston spied a knife in its scabbard on the wall. He grabbed its carved ivory handle.

"I wouldn't do that," the Tulku advised.

Cranston whipped out the knife. He started to go for the boy. Then he froze.

The knife was quivering as if alive. He stared down at it. He saw the carved face on the handle turn, growl—*and sink its teeth into his wrist!*

Cranston screamed. He screamed again as the knife flew out of his hand. It slashed his thigh. Then it went for his face.

Cranston jerked his head to the side. The blade only sliced his cheek as it zipped by. It buried itself in the wall. Quivering, it came to rest.

Cranston lay on the ground, clutching his bleeding leg.

"Am I in hell?" he moaned.

"Not yet," the Tulku said. "But you have to go through it—to find your way out."

Chapter 3

Dr. Roy Tam knew how to survive in New York City. He minded his own business. Tonight, though, the Asian-American scientist had broken that rule. And it was going to cost him his life.

He was coming home late from his laboratory when he heard a groan coming from an alley. He decided to have a look. Someone might need his help.

Wrong decision.

Three thugs stood in the alley. At their feet was a dead policemen. Tam saw them all. And all three saw him.

The thugs took him to an East River bridge. Through breaks in the fog, he saw dark water swirling below.

Tam would have made a run for it. But his feet were encased in cement.

All he could do was beg, "Please. I have a family. I won't talk, I promise you."

The first thug, Maxie, answered, "I know you won't."

He joined his buddy, English Johnny, in hoisting Tam up over the railing. Their partner, Duke Rollins, looked on, bored.

"I hate this heavy lifting," Johnny complained.

Tam started to scream. But he knew he was wasting his breath. The streets were empty. There was no one to hear, no one to help.

Suddenly a sound drowned out his scream—then choked it off.

"Heh-heh-heh-heh-heh!"

It was the sound of a laugh. Not a happy one, though. It was a hideous laugh. It filled the air. And chilled the blood.

The thugs stopped in mid-hoist.

"What was that?" said Maxie, his hand going to his shoulder holster.

The laugh sounded again.

"Who's there?" Duke shouted. "Show yourself, fella, or I'll give it to you good!"

A deep voice boomed out. "You murdered a policeman, Duke."

The thugs' eyes swiveled like pinballs gone

wild. But all they saw was the dark night.

Again they heard the voice. "The weed of crime bears bitter fruit."

Maxie turned to Duke. Panic twisted his tongue. "This ain't good. Diamond Bert told me about a couple mugs that got tagged by some guy at South Street Seaport. They couldn't even *see* him!"

"Shut your hole," Duke snapped. "Diamond Bert's out of his skull."

Again the voice spoke. "Did you think you'd get away with it? Did you think *I* wouldn't know?"

"Think you're smart, don't you, friend?" Duke said, pulling out his revolver. "Well, take this!"

He emptied his gun, firing in all directions.

The shots were still echoing when the laugh came back to mock him.

Snarling, Duke ran for the car. From the front seat he pulled out his answer to that laugh. A submachine gun. He opened up with it. The other thugs hit the deck, pulling Tam down with them. Bullets made Swiss cheese of the air.

The salvo was followed by silence.

"You got him, Duke," Maxie said, getting to his feet. "You filled him full of holes."

"You're sure as shooting right I—" Duke started to say.

That was as far as he got. His smile vanished as his head snapped back. He fell backward, landing hard on the bridge.

"Duke, what you doing?" said Maxie, while Johnny stood with his mouth hanging open.

Duke scrambled to his feet. His fists flailed out in all directions. *Thunk!* He doubled over, clutching his belly. *Crack!* His head snapped back again. Then his jacket bunched up around his neck. Something was lifting him off the ground. His feet pedaled in empty air as the voice spoke.

"You've committed murder, Duke. Now you're going to confess to it."

"Says who?" Duke snarled.

Duke sailed through the air. He crash-landed on the pavement. He shook his head to clear it.

"You will confess," the voice told him. "Because if you don't, I'll be there. You can never escape me. No more than you can escape your guilty conscience."

"You don't scare me," Duke declared.

"Here we go again," the voice said, almost sighing.

Duke was yanked up, used as a punching bag,

dragged along the bridge railing. Dangling in the air above the river, he gasped, "I'll do it! I'll do it! I'll confess!"

"You'll go to the police station on Second Avenue," the voice told him. "You will surrender yourself to Sergeant Noonan. And you will do it *now*."

With that, Duke was hurled through the open door of his car. He lay in a moaning, bloody heap in the front seat.

Again the laugh sounded, stronger than ever.

By now, Maxie and Johnny had forgotten about Tam. All they could think about was getting out of there fast. But they stopped in their tracks.

They saw a shadow at their feet. It stretched down the pavement before them. Their eyes followed the shadow to its source. A man stood on the bridge, blocking their way. A black cloak shrouded his body. A black slouch hat was pulled low over his eyes. And that terrible laugh came from his unsmiling lips.

He didn't have to say a word. The two thugs knew what he wanted them to do. They didn't argue.

They jumped in the car, shoving aside their pitiful pal to make room. They gunned the engine and raced off. But they weren't making an escape. They were heading straight for the Second Avenue police station.

Meanwhile Tam lay helpless, shivering with fear. His shivers turned violent as the man in black came toward him.

"Please don't!" Tam groaned, as the man pulled out two silver .45 automatics.

Tam shut his eyes as the shots rang out.

Slowly he opened them. The concrete around his feet had been blasted away.

He knew he should say thank you. But there was something he had to say first.

"Who *are* you?"

Chapter 4

A taxi glided out of the fog like a ghost. There was nothing ghostly about the driver, though. He looked solid as a rock. A rock you could chip and scratch but never crack. The kind of rock that New York was built on.

His name was on the license on his dashboard, next to a picture of his wife. Moe Shrevnitz.

Moe watched as Tam slid into the backseat, followed by the man in black. He looked at Tam's face in his rearview mirror. Tam was frightened and confused. Moe smiled to himself. He had felt that way, too, the first time he met the man in black. Before he learned who that man was. Before the menace was taken out of the mystery. And he came to know the man as—

The Shadow.

Tam glanced sideways at The Shadow. But he

caught only a hint of the face under the low slouched hat.

"I want to thank you," Tam said. He got no answer. He cleared his throat. "Uh, you fellas must be busy. Just drop me anywhere."

Then The Shadow spoke. "You're Dr. Roy Tam. You teach science at New York University."

"Yes," Tam said, startled.

"I've saved your life, Roy Tam," The Shadow said. "Now it belongs to me."

"It does?" Tam said. "What do you mean?"

"You'll become my agent, like many others all over the world," The Shadow told him. "Some carry out missions for me every day. Others carry out just one in their whole lives. But they are lives with purpose. Purpose and honor."

He looked Tam straight in the eyes. Tam felt all questions fade. All he could do was ask, "Could I, uh—ask my wife about this?"

"No," The Shadow said.

Tam swallowed hard. "Okay."

By now the taxi had speeded up. Moe Shrevnitz drove like a demon.

The Shadow spoke quickly. "You'll go through your life as always. If I ever need your help, I'll contact you. When you hear one of my agents say,

20

'The sun is shining,' you'll answer, 'But the ice is slippery.' That will identify you to each other. Then you'll await my instructions. Understand?"

"Right," said Tam, nodding.

"Remember," The Shadow went on, "I demand one thing from my agents. Obedience. Absolute, unquestioning obedience."

Tam looked into The Shadow's dark eyes. "Okay. Yeah. Sure. No problem." Tam leaned forward. "But tell me one thing—how did you know what was happening to me? How did you know who I am?"

A chill ran through Tam this time when he heard The Shadow's laugh. He shuddered at The Shadow's words, *"The Shadow knows."*

The brakes screeched. The cab skidded to a stop. Moe Shrevnitz got out of the front seat when Tam got out of the back. He stood with Tam on the sidewalk.

"That's...that's *The Shadow*," Tam said.

"Hey, you're a pretty smart guy," Moe said with a grin. He held out his hand to shake hands with Tam.

"I've heard the rumors—in the papers, on the radio," Tam said, shaking hands. "But I didn't think the guy actually *existed*."

"He *doesn't*. Get it?" Moe said, tightening his grip.

Moe wouldn't let Tam go until he nodded.

Tam looked down at his hand. Moe had slipped a ring onto his finger. A small ring with a bright red gem in its center. Moe held his own hand up. The glow from a streetlight glinted off an identical ring on Moe's finger.

"Don't ever take it off," Moe said, and turned to get back into his cab.

"Wait a minute," Tam said. "Who are you?"

"Somebody just like you," Moe said, jabbing his finger into Tam's chest. "Somebody who owes him his life."

Tam could still feel that sharp jab as he watched the cab roar off. Then he slowly headed for his house. "The sun is shining—but the ice is slippery," he repeated to himself. He would be ready for The Shadow's summons.

Meanwhile, Moe was racing uptown. The Shadow was running behind schedule.

Or rather Lamont Cranston was.

The man in the back of the cab had changed out of his black clothes and tucked them away. He now wore a tuxedo. His face, though, was pale and sweating above his gleaming white shirt.

"You okay, boss?" Moe asked. He knew that jobs like this took something out of the man he served.

"I'll be fine by the time we get to the Cobalt Club," Cranston said. "Better step on it. My uncle will be furious. He likes to think his time is valuable. Not that I've delayed his dinner, though. *Nothing* would make my uncle put off his dinner."

Cranston was right. By the time he joined his uncle, Wainright Barth was finishing his meal. He was sinking his silver fork into the last piece of bloody rare meat on his china plate.

"Sorry I'm late, Uncle Wainright," Cranston said. "There was a little accident on the bridge."

"I'm not upset about *that*," Wainright Barth declared.

"Then what *are* you upset about?" Cranston asked. He didn't sound very interested in the answer.

Nonetheless, his uncle gave it to him loud and clear. "Hadley Richardson is one of New York's top financial advisers. I had to pull a lot of strings to get you a meeting with him. And you didn't even show up."

But Cranston wasn't listening. He was looking

at a woman who had just entered the Cobalt Club. And he was not the only one. Almost every man in the fancy supper club was looking at her.

She was beautiful.

Wainright Barth, though, hadn't even noticed her.

"Lamont, are you listening to what I'm saying?" he demanded.

"Right. Sure," Cranston said. Reluctantly he returned to the conversation. "Where were we?"

Wainright Barth sighed. "Lamont, I have never meddled in your affairs. Even when you disappeared for seven years, I didn't ask questions. But this is different. You are in charge of the entire Cranston estate. All your living relatives depend on money from it."

"Including you, right?" Cranston couldn't resist saying.

"That's not the point," Barth said. "You simply can't be trusted to make investments alone. Look at that crazy stock you just bought. What was it? IBT? IBS?"

"IBM," Cranston said.

"'International Business Machines,'" said Barth, shaking his head. "Well, that's a crackpot company if I ever saw one."

"Let's just say I have a hunch," Cranston said.

Barth sighed. "Lamont, you never listen to me. I don't know *why* you keep calling me for dinner."

Cranston didn't have to think of an answer to that question. A bellboy came to the table looking for his uncle.

"Police Commissioner Barth?" the bellboy asked. Barth nodded, and the boy handed him a message on a silver tray. "This just came by telephone, sir."

Barth read it. He gave an annoyed grunt.

"So what's new in the cops and robbers business?" asked Cranston.

"It's that blasted Shadow again," said Barth.

"I thought you said he was just a rumor," said Cranston, giving his uncle a big smile.

Barth held up the message. "That's not what Duke Rollins said tonight."

"Duke Rollins?" said Cranston.

"A crook we've been after. He walked right into a police station and confessed to a murder with two of his pals. He kept babbling about The Shadow. You know what? I'm going to form a task force to find out who this character is."

Still smiling, Cranston leaned back into the shadows and looked deep into his uncle's eyes.

There was no smile in Cranston's voice. It was deep and harsh. It was the voice that the killers had heard on the bridge that night.

"You're not going to form a task force."

"Ah, forget about the task force," Barth decided.

"You are not going to pay attention to reports of The Shadow," his nephew commanded.

"I'm going to ignore those absurd reports," Barth declared.

"There is no Shadow," Cranston said.

"If there's a Shadow, I'm Eleanor Roosevelt," the Police Commissioner proclaimed.

Still smiling, Cranston broke off eye contact with his uncle.

Barth shook his head. "Sorry—where was I?" he said shakily.

"You were about to tell me who that woman is," Cranston said. "The one who just came into the club. I have a hunch about her—an even bigger one than IBM."

Chapter 5

Margo Lane was beautiful and bored. She was bored with men falling in love with her. They panted like puppy dogs, begging for scraps of affection. She was bored with the Cobalt Club. The menu never changed. She was bored with nights like this. She would see the same old people, say the same old things.

Margo hailed a waiter.

"Waiter, may I have a glass of—" she began.

"Mouton Rothschild, 1928," the waiter said. The bottle of rare French wine was already in his hands. He poured Margo a glassful.

"Why, yes," Margo said. "But how—?"

"From the gentleman," the waiter said.

"Gentleman?" Margo said.

"Lamont Cranston," said a voice behind her. "May I sit down?"

Margo looked up at him. She felt many different things. She was attracted to him. He was definitely a handsome guy. She was frightened of him. There was something dangerous in his dark eyes. She was curious about him. How could he read her mind?

But one thing she knew for sure—she was no longer bored.

"Please, do sit down," she said.

Cranston took the seat opposite her. But before they could start talking, Chad Martin arrived.

Chad was one of the many annoying men who insisted on being in love with Margo. There was no getting rid of him. Now he was insisting she go to a jazz club with him.

Lamont Cranston cleared his throat. Chad looked at him for the first time. Their eyes met.

Chad's face went blank. He turned back to Margo.

"Louis Armstrong may be at the club tonight, and Earl Hines," he said. At the same time, he picked up the bottle of wine the waiter had left. Before Margo's startled eyes, he poured the wine onto the front of his trousers.

"*Chad*! What are you *doing*?" Margo exclaimed.

Chad looked down at his pants.

"Oh my gosh," he gasped. Red-faced, he made a dash for the men's room.

Margo turned back to Lamont Cranston. His face was expressionless. She had no idea what he was thinking.

"I wonder what made Chad do that?" Margo said. She gave Cranston a searching look.

Cranston shrugged. "Some guys will do anything for a laugh." Then he leaned forward toward Margo. "But let's get down to serious business. What do you want for dinner? As for myself, I have a sudden craving for Peking duck."

Margo gazed at him in disbelief. He had done it again. "Odd that you should say that," she said. "I was thinking the same thing."

"Funny coincidence," Cranston commented.

"Very funny," Margo agreed.

"But a lucky one, too," Cranston went on. "I know a great Chinese restaurant. Best Peking duck in town. Will you join me?"

"I'd be happy to," Margo said. "I can hardly wait to find out what else you know. I can see this is going to be a very educational evening."

"I hope so," Cranston said, getting up from the table.

"I hope we can find a cab," Margo said, following him. "It's getting pretty late."

"Don't worry," Cranston said. "I feel lucky tonight."

Margo was not surprised when a cab appeared the moment they left the club. She was starting to think that nothing about Lamont Cranston would surprise her.

It seemed almost natural that the cabdriver knew where to go before Cranston told him. Or that he left his meter off during the whole trip to Chinatown. Or that he only accepted a ten-dollar bill after Cranston gave him a sharp look and then glanced at Margo.

She wasn't even surprised when Cranston talked with the waiter in the man's native tongue.

"You know Chinese?" Margo said, wanting to find out more about this mysterious yet fascinating man.

"Just Mandarin, that's all," Cranston said.

"You must have a very interesting past," Margo pressed on.

"Oh, just the usual thing," Cranston said. "Boarding school. College. Military service in the war. A bit of traveling afterward. And now, tending the family fortune, trying to make it grow. About as interesting as potato farming, I'm afraid."

By now his hand had settled over Margo's. Margo smiled, and turned it palm up.

"You don't mind me doing a bit of palm reading, do you?" she said. "It's a hobby."

Cranston stiffened. Then he forced himself to relax. "Go ahead," he said. "I'm afraid you'll be disappointed, though."

Margo was already studying his palm. Her brow furrowed. "You have a strange life line. It splits right down the middle. That usually means secrets. Do you have any secrets? Guilty secrets?"

"One or two," Cranston admitted. "Doesn't everyone?"

"But yours look very troubling," said Margo.

Cranston pulled his hand away. At the same time his eyes met hers.

After a moment, Margo put her hand to her forehead.

"What's the matter—a headache?" asked Cranston.

"Not really," Margo said. "It's more like a—"

"A buzzing?" Cranston suggested. He leaned forward. "Like radio static?"

"Yes. Yes, exactly. But it's clearing up now," Margo said. She shook her head. "You're a strange man. You know what wine I like. What food I like. What I'm feeling. Is there anything you don't know?"

Cranston smiled. "What the future holds for us two. But maybe we can start finding that out tonight."

At that moment, the waiter arrived with their food. They didn't return to the subject of their future until after dinner, when Cranston saw Margo to her door.

"Thank you," Margo said. "I had a wonderful time."

"I'm not sure I can recall an evening as exciting as this one," Cranston agreed.

"Shall we do it again?" Margo said.

She was taken aback to see Cranston hesitate before he said, "Yes. Let's."

He held out his hand. Margo shook hands with him. They turned away from each other.

Suddenly they turned to stand face to face again. It was as if they were connected by an invisible rubber band. Their arms went around each other in an embrace. Their lips met.

Again Margo was taken aback. It was Cranston who broke off their kiss.

"Good night, Miss Lane," he said.

"Good night, Mr. Cranston," Margo said. She watched him climb into the waiting cab—the same one that had driven them to the restaurant.

Inside the cab, Moe Shrevnitz said, "I like her, boss. She's different than your usual dames."

"Yes," said Cranston. But his voice was worried. "More different than she knows. Maybe too different." His mouth tightened. "I don't think I'll see her again."

"But *why*?" Moe asked.

"She has powers that she is unaware of," Cranston said. "Dangerous powers."

"Dangerous?" said Moe. "For who?"

"For me, Moe," Cranston said. "For me."

Chapter 6

"I have to forget her," Lamont Cranston told himself. *"Wipe her out of my mind. I could never relax around her. Never let down my guard. I could look into her mind—but she might look into mine as well. She might see things that no one should see. Things I don't even want to see myself."*

He was sitting before the dying fire in the great stone fireplace in his mansion. He couldn't sleep. Perhaps he was afraid to. Afraid he would dream of this woman he had to forget.

He stared into the orange flames.

And suddenly Margo Lane *was* forgotten.

Before his eyes, the flames leapt up. They exploded into a fireball. In the heart of the burning sphere appeared a face. And that face was not Margo's.

It was a man's face. A face from Asia. But

Cranston barely noticed the high cheekbones, the cruel mouth. The eyes were what captivated him.

Margo might disturb Cranston's peace of mind. But those burning eyes were a real threat. They made Cranston's mind feel as if it were melting.

Who was the man with those eyes? Where was he? What did he want?

Cranston knew he would find out. He would not even have to look for this man. This man would hunt him down. It was his fate.

Cranston stood up and went to the window. He looked out at the city, cloaked in darkness. Somewhere out there evil lurked. And not even The Shadow knew what it was.

The Shadow wasn't the only one that night to sense an unknown evil. Isaac Newboldt did, too.

Newboldt ran the Museum of Asian Antiquities. He had no special mental powers. He just had a sixty-year-old head stuffed full of history. But as he stared at the coffin delivered to his museum, he sensed something creepy about it. More than creepy. He felt something sinister.

Berger, his assistant, had phoned Newboldt in the dead of the night. He told Newboldt that an unexpected shipment had arrived. Newboldt had to come in and examine it right away. He was rubbing sleep out of his eyes when he entered the museum on Central Park West. He yawned walking past rows of menacing statues of Asian warriors in the dark rooms. He arrived at the brightly lit loading dock in the rear. The coffin gleamed in its opened shipping case. Suddenly he was wide awake.

"First I figured I'd label it a mummy case, since it came from Tibet," Berger said.

"Mummy cases come from Egypt, Berger," Newboldt told him.

"Yeah. Right," said Berger. "I thought of that. Besides, it's metal. So it's a sarcophagus."

"No," Newboldt said. He tried to keep the edge out of his voice. Berger was an idiot. For the money the museum paid, help was hard to get. "Tibetan sarcophagi are stone. What happened to the truckers who dropped it off?"

"Gone," Berger said. "They took off without even making me sign for it."

"Stranger and stranger," said Newboldt. "Well, it's obviously a mistake. We'll have to find out how to return it."

"Right," Berger said. He looked around for the guard. "I'll have the crate lid put back on."

"Still, it wouldn't hurt to take a look at it," Newboldt said, moving closer. "It does look rather interesting."

His eyes drank in the beautifully made coffin. Delicate engraving decorated its top. Along one side ran hinges for the lid. Along the other side ran a row of latches to keep the lid shut.

Newboldt ran his hand along the top. He buffed it with a corner of his sleeve. The metal shone brightly. "It's solid silver!" he exclaimed.

Newboldt spoke to the guard lounging in the doorway. "Nelson! Take the sides off this crate!"

Nelson took a last bite of an apple he was munching. He stuffed the core in his pocket and picked up a crowbar. He pried away the rest of the crate while Newboldt waited impatiently.

Finally the coffin stood free. Newboldt peered at the engraving. "It's writing," he said.

"What kind?" said Berger, looking over his shoulder.

"Latin," Newboldt said.

"What does it say?" asked Berger.

"You don't know Latin?" said Newboldt.

Berger shrugged. "It's all Greek to me."

Inwardly Newboldt groaned. Then he translated. "'The Kha Khan. The power of God on

earth. The Seal of the Emperor of Mankind.'"
Newboldt looked up in wonder. "Temujin! This is
the silver coffin of Temujin!"

"Who's Temujin?" inquired Berger, scratching
his head.

"A man who very nearly conquered the globe
seven centuries ago," said Newboldt. He stepped
back from the coffin. He gazed at it in total awe.

"So how come I haven't heard of him?" Berger
wanted to know.

"Temujin was the birth name of—Genghis
Khan," Newboldt told him.

That made not only Berger but Nelson stiffen.
Even the guard had heard of the ancient Mongol
ruler—the most ruthless conqueror of all time.

"What did you say the shipper's name was?"
Newboldt demanded of Berger.

"The label just said Tibet," Berger said.

"I'm going to make a phone call," Newboldt
said. He didn't want Berger to see that the coffin
was starting to make him shudder.

Berger took a look at the coffin. He didn't feel
like being around it, either.

"I'll go help you," he announced.

Before they left, Newboldt spoke sharply to the
guard. "Nelson! Whatever you do, don't open it!"

"No *sir*," Nelson said, his hand on his gun.

"*Don't open it. Don't open it,*" Nelson kept repeating to himself as he stood guard. His hand was on his gun. Nobody was going to open this coffin. Good jobs were hard to find. Nobody was going to make him lose this one.

He heard a noise. A scratching noise. His eyes whipped around the platform. There was nobody here but him.

He heard the scratching again. Then he realized where it was coming from. *Inside* the coffin.

There was a loud click as one of the latches of the lid snapped open.

Gun in hand, Nelson dashed for the coffin. With his free hand, he slammed the latch shut.

But at the other end of the coffin, two more latches snapped open. As he lunged to shut them, the first snapped open again. He stuck his gun in his holster and ran around the coffin, slamming latches shut. It was a race—and he lost. Panting, he could only draw his gun again as the lid swung open.

From inside the coffin a man stood up. He was clothed in gold and silk fabric encrusted with jewels.

One man had already seen his face that night.

And that man was Lamont Cranston.

Now Nelson saw it. That face. And those eyes. He tried to fight the power of those eyes.

His hand tightened on his gun. "Hey, Mister, we're closed," he growled.

"I am Shiwan Khan," the stranger said, stepping out of the coffin. "Join me or die."

"What?" gasped Nelson.

"Join me or die," Shiwan Khan repeated, taking a step toward Nelson.

"This is—this is private property," said Nelson, forcing the words past the lump in his throat. "Don't come any—any—"

His finger tightened on the trigger. At least Nelson tried to make it happen. But somehow he'd lost control of himself.

"Your mind is weak," the stranger said. "Fall to your knees."

What a nutty idea, Nelson thought. Before he knew it, he was on his knees.

Newboldt and Berger were on their way back to the loading dock when they heard the shot.

They hurried to the dock. They found the guard's dead body there.

"What happened?" cried Newboldt, crouching over Nelson's body. "Who did this?"

He looked frantically around the dock for a clue. He saw nothing. He saw nobody.

His mind was too clouded to see Shiwan Khan standing right there in front of him.

Newboldt couldn't see Shiwan Khan's triumphant face. Khan was enjoying this new world he'd come to conquer.

Chapter 7

The next day, cops swarmed around the museum. Even Police Commissioner Wainright Barth was there. The murder was sure to make headlines. The man who caught the killer would make the front pages, too. The trouble was, the cops didn't have a clue who did it.

"Weird," said Barth. He scratched his head as he looked at the corpse.

"Definitely weird," agreed Inspector Cardona, the officer in charge of the case. He shook his head, looking at the empty coffin.

Neither of them noticed a cop making notes on the crime scene. There was no reason to. He was just an ordinary cop, doing his job.

There was one unusual thing about him, though. This big, tough cop was wearing a small ring. A ring with a bright red stone.

No one gave the cop a second glance as he

slipped away from the scene. The case was going nowhere fast. Cops were leaving for coffee breaks.

This cop, though, wasn't taking a break. He had a job to do.

The job took him downtown in his squad car. He entered a run-down office building. He stopped in front of a grimy glass door. It was marked "B. Jonas." He peered inside. The room was bare. This was still the right place.

He put his note into an envelope from his breast pocket. The envelope had no address. It was just marked with a silhouette. The silhouette of a man in a slouch hat and a cloak.

He dropped the envelope through the mail slot in the door. *Whoosh*—it was sucked inside. The cop headed back uptown. He had completed his job.

The cop knew who was going to get his message. The guy who once had saved his life. But he didn't know how it would get to him.

Luther Burbank did. He'd designed the spider-web of tubes that ran all over the city. He'd spent millions of dollars to lay them down, and even more to disguise them. He'd used hundreds of skilled workers. The money wasn't his, of course. It came from the Cranston fortune. And he didn't have to pay the workers. They worked for free, paying off a debt. They all wore rings with bright red stones.

Burbank had one of those rings on his finger as he waited in the center of the spiderweb. Tubes wound their way over the walls, floor, and ceiling of the room where he sat. All tubes ended here, within his reach. Through them, high-pressure air bore messages in minutes from all over town.

The only light shone on a map of New York that covered a wall. Pins marked every tube entry in the city. On Burbank's desk was the best radio transmitter money could buy. And next to it was a device with a red button.

Burbank pressed the button the moment he read the latest message.

Lamont Cranston was getting dressed in his mansion. He saw the red light flashing in his ring. He grabbed his coat and was out the door in a flash.

Minutes later, Moe Shrevnitz arrived with his cab. Moe's ring had flashed, too.

Cranston didn't waste time with words. "The Sanctum," he said.

"You got it," Moe said.

Moe drove to Times Square. Cranston got out.

He wove through tourists taking in the town and hustlers out to take advantage of them. He went down an alley where not even the craziest tourist would go. He looked over his shoulder to make sure no one had followed. Then he pressed three bricks, one after another, on the dead-end wall.

The wall opened up—just wide enough for him to slip through. It closed behind him as he went along a narrow corridor. He went down an even narrower stairway. He came to a thick steel door. He opened the combination lock and entered, closing the door tightly behind him.

The Shadow was in his Sanctum.

The walls were covered with books on every subject. The Shadow had to know a great deal about a great many things. On a desk was a radio transmitter—the same kind as Burbank had.

The Shadow snapped it on. He spoke into its microphone. "Report."

He heard Burbank's voice. "Our agent in the Twenty-sixth Precinct reports a murder at the Museum of Asian Antiquities. Agent advises inquiry."

"Murder," muttered the Shadow. He snapped off the set and moved toward the door.

Then he stopped dead in his tracks.

The steel door had swung wide open.

Someone stood in the doorway.

A figure dressed in gold and silk with gleaming jewels.

Shiwan Khan looked Cranston up and down.

"Hmm. I thought you would be taller," Khan said.

"Who are you?" Cranston demanded.

Khan smiled. "Shiwan Kahn, last descendant of Genghis Khan. I am sure you are deeply honored." His smile widened. "Don't bother introducing yourself. I know who you are. Who you *really* are." Khan bowed. "Ying Ko. I am a great admirer."

"Ying Ko?" Cranston managed to keep his voice calm. "Who's he?"

Khan's lip curled. "Please. I can invade your mind as easily as I can enter this room. May I sit down?"

Without waiting for an answer, Khan made himself comfortable on the desk. "You're hurting my feelings, Ying Ko," he continued. "I thought you would enjoy meeting another man who can cloud men's minds so they cannot see."

"You were a student of the Tulku?" Cranston said. He couldn't believe it. The Tulku was all that was good in the world. And Cranston could see already that Khan was all that was evil.

"Yes, I was—his last student," Khan said. "But not his prize one. That was you. He spoke of you constantly. I'm afraid I was—a failure. Not that I didn't learn the tricks he had to teach. But I decided not to use them the way he wanted."

Khan paused. He touched his throat with a long fingernail. "Talk makes my throat dry. Do you have a drink? I'd be glad to pay for it." He pulled out a silver coin. "I know you don't need the money. But you have none like this. It's a collector's item—from my private mint."

"Be my guest," Cranston said. He took a bottle from his desk and poured Khan a drink. It was a good way to loosen Khan's tongue.

"Did you happen to visit a museum last night?" Cranston asked, after Khan tossed back his drink in a gulp.

Cranston refilled Khan's glass.

"It had a wonderful collection of Tibetan tapestries," Khan said. He took a long sip, and smiled at Cranston. "Ah, Ying Ko. Grown men in Tibet still shiver at your name. You are my idol. I studied your triumphs. Do you remember the raid you led on the village of Barga?"

Cranston couldn't stop a flash of memory from lighting up his eyes.

"I see you do recall it," Khan said.

"It—rings a bell," Cranston admitted.

"It was a master stroke," Khan said. "Swift. Vicious. Sudden. What genius."

"Uh huh," said Cranston. He wanted to change the subject. "So what brings you to the Big Apple?"

"My destiny," Khan said, emptying his glass. "Genghis Khan conquered half the world. I will finish the job."

Cranston poured him another drink. "And how do you plan to do that?"

Khan rolled his eyes. "If I told you, it wouldn't be a surprise." He took a sip of his drink. "I traveled here in Genghis Khan's holy crypt to absorb his power. In three days, it will be the date of his death in the Year of the Swine. Then the entire world will hear my roar. It will surrender to the new emperor of Sianking." He sipped again. "Nice tie you're wearing. Where did you get it?"

"Brooks Brothers," said Cranston. "But it's not your style. You're a barbarian."

Khan's eyes looked into his. *We both are,* Khan hissed. "I know that inside you beats a heart of darkness. You dip into it every time you put on your hat and cloak." He grabbed Cranston by the wrist. "Join me. You are Ying Ko, the Butcher of Lhasa. You, and only you, deserve to be by my side. Your hands still long to wash themselves in blood. Your mouth still waters at *real* power. Be my partner, Ying Ko."

Cranston broke free. He backed away until his back was to the wall.

"That's not my name anymore," Cranston said.

"But it's who you still are," said Khan.

With the back of his foot, Cranston kicked a wall panel. It opened. He whipped a .45 automatic from the hiding place.

Khan didn't blink. He merely spun the coin in his hand high into the air.

Cranston could not help himself. His eyes followed the dazzling blur.

When he tore his eyes away, Khan was gone.

But Khan's voice echoed through the Sanctum.

"We'll meet again—soon."

Chapter 8

Dr. Roy Tam sat with his family at the breakfast table. The radio was playing. Tam's wife sipped a second cup of coffee. Tam's boy, Tommy, munched cornflakes while doing last-minute homework. Tam was reading the morning paper. Suddenly Tam lowered the paper and listened hard to what the radio newsman was saying.

"Good morning, Mr. and Mrs. America. Another report of The Shadow. The same Shadow the police have chased for five years!"

By now Mrs. Tam and Tommy were listening, too. Everyone was interested in the mysterious Shadow.

"This latest eerie episode took place on a Manhattan bridge late last night. Three witnesses actually saw the event take place," the newscaster went on. "Some say this Shadow is a foe to all evildoers. But others fear that The Shadow is himself evil. What do you think, Radioland?"

Tommy declared, "My teacher says they just made up The Shadow so we'd listen to the radio more. It that true, Dad?"

Tam cleared his throat. "No, it's...well, *may*be...I mean, how should I know..."

A knock sounded on the door.

"I'll get it," Tam said, leaping up.

He went through the living room and opened the front door. It was Lamont Cranston. But to Tam, Lamont Cranston was a complete stranger.

Cranston held up his hand. Tam saw a ring with a red stone.

"The sun is shining," Cranston said.

Tam swallowed hard, and answered, "But the ice is slippery."

Cranston nodded. Tam joined him on the stoop, closing the door behind him.

"You're an agent of The Shadow?" Tam whispered.

"Who?" Cranston replied.

"Right. Gotcha," Tam said with a wink. "What do you want?"

"A metal analysis," Cranston said.

"You came to the right man," Tam said.

"I know," Cranston assured him, pulling out

the only clue that Khan had left. The strange coin from Khan's private mint.

It was even stranger than Cranston imagined. Tam and Cranston worked in Tam's laboratory all day and into the night trying to find out what it was.

At last they did. In Tam's final test, he dropped the coin into a dish of water. The water vanished in a single puff.

Tam looked up, his eyes full of wonder. "Bronzium! This metal is bronzium! I didn't think it existed. But here it is!"

"And what is bronzium?" Cranston asked.

"The ancient Chinese said it was the very stuff the universe was formed of," Tam said. He gazed at the coin with awe. "Where did it come from?"

"I believe from Sianking," Cranston said.

"Makes sense," said Tam. "Legend says that Sianking was the birthplace of the world."

Cranston's eyes narrowed. "Could bronzium be used for making some kind of weapon?"

Tam hesitated. He thought a moment. "Theoretically, yes," he said, finally.

"How?" asked Cranston. There was an edge of urgency in his voice.

"The molecules in the metal are unstable,"

said Tam. "The bonds holding them together are weak. If those bonds were broken, the molecules might collide and split, releasing enormous amounts of energy."

"An explosion?" Cranston asked.

Tam nodded grimly.

"How big?" Cranston demanded.

Tam bit his lip. "No man can say. The breakdown would spread to all levels of the molecule's atomic construction. You could call it an implosive/explosive submolecular device."

"Or an atomic bomb," Cranston suggested.

"Catchy," Tam said. "But fortunately, it's a lot easier said than done. In fact, I'd say it's impossible. First you'd need a beryllium sphere to contain the mechanism, and nobody is even dreaming of making one of those. But even more important, you'd need a genius or even a team of geniuses to design the mechanism itself."

"What would it look like?" Cranston asked.

Tam went to a blackboard.

"It would have some kind of shell," he said, making a sketch. "With tiny but powerful charges spaced regularly over its surface. Something like *this*."

Tam stepped back. "This is just a rough idea, of

course. As I said, such a device doesn't exist. And I pray it never will."

"You and me both," Cranston said. Then he looked at his watch. "I have to go now. I'm late for a date. Thanks for your help."

"Anytime," Tam assured him. "I'll always owe The Shadow."

Even with Moe running red lights, Cranston was late again for dinner at the Cobalt Club.

"Know what puzzles me, Lamont?" his uncle Wainwright asked. "How a man with nothing to do can be late for every engagement."

"Practice, Uncle," said Cranston, signaling a waiter for a menu.

At that moment, Barth turned even more sour. "Blast it. It's that Lane woman again."

Cranston turned to see Margo Lane heading for their table.

"She's been pestering me all day. I had to practically hide under my—" He broke the sentence off as Margo arrived. He gave her a big smile. "Hello, Miss Lane. Delightful to—"

"You can drop the act, Commissioner Barth," Margo snapped, putting her hands on her hips. "What have you done about my father?"

"I told you, there's nothing we can do, unless—"

"Unless he blows himself up?" Margo demanded.

Cranston motioned to the chair beside him. "Won't you sit down, Miss Lane?" he asked.

Margo glared at the commissioner. "Why thank you, Mr. Cranston," she said, taking a seat.

Barth gave his nephew a murderous glance, then faced Margo again.

"Miss Lane," Barth said, "the police can't act just because your father is acting strangely."

"It's more than that," Margo insisted. "He's *always* acted strangely. He's the original absent-minded scientist. He can't even tell you if he's got on a red shirt or a green one. But now he's refusing to see me."

"Well, he is working for the War Department," Barth said. "His work is probably top secret. Maybe even dangerous."

"No, his project is harmless," Margo said. "It's some kind of energy research. He's been tinkering with the same funny-looking device for a year now. I once asked him what it was. He answered me with a bunch of technical gibberish."

Cranston thought a moment, then leaned forward. "You've seen this device?" he asked.

"Every time I visit Dad at the lab," Margo said. "He practically lives there."

"And it looks kind of strange?"

"Really strange," said Margo. She pulled a pen from her purse and made a quick drawing on a napkin.

Cranston looked at the drawing and stiffened. It wasn't exactly like Tam's sketch. But it was close enough.

"So you think there's something wrong?" he asked, ignoring his uncle's warning look.

"I *know* there's something wrong," Margo said. "I called him over the phone. And he spoke to me in *Chinese*."

"Odd," said Cranston.

"Odder than you think," Margo said. "He doesn't *know* Chinese." She turned to Barth. "Commissioner, I insist that—"

Barth sighed. "All right, all right. I'll have a policeman drop by his lab tomorrow."

"But tomorrow may be too late," Margo said. "Mr. Cranston, can't you make your uncle—"

Then she stopped. Cranston had already left the table. He was halfway out of the club.

Margo quickly rose from the table and caught up with him as he went out the door.

"Wait a minute," she said. "What's wrong? I thought last night we—"

Their eyes met again. This time Cranston did not look away. Neither did Margo.

"Your eyes," Margo gasped.

"I have to go," Cranston said.

"Ying Ko!" Margo exclaimed.

Then she stepped back, shaking her head. "Who is Ying Ko?" she said, puzzled.

Cranston's eyes burned into hers. His voice was deep as night. *"You'll forget me!"* he said.

"Why would I do that?" Margo asked, even more puzzled. "Look, Mr. Cranston, I don't know what kind of women you're used to, but—"

Cranston heaved a sigh of relief as Moe drove up. He needed a fast getaway. Margo was more dangerous than he thought. More dangerous than he imagined any woman could be.

But he couldn't spend time worrying about that now.

He had an even greater danger on his hands. A danger ticking like a bomb set to go off.

Chapter 9

Moe Shrevnitz had seen it happen before. But it still made him queasy.

He heard heavy, rasping breaths from the back of his cab. They came from Lamont Cranston. Cranston sounded like a runner after a race.

He saw Cranston's face in the rearview mirror. It was a picture of pain.

Moe could not stand watching it. He looked away.

When he looked back, Cranston was gone. In his place was a man in a black cloak and slouch hat.

"The Federal Building," The Shadow said.

Moe wondered what The Shadow wanted there. But it wasn't his job to know what The Shadow was doing. It was enough for Moe that *The Shadow knew*.

But even The Shadow didn't know what he'd

find in the laboratory of Margo's father, Dr. Reinhardt Lane.

Dr. Lane was still in the lab. But he was getting ready to leave. The device he was working on was in a carrying case. He was buttoning up his overcoat.

Dr. Lane's eyes were blank. So was his mind. All he could hear was the voice that he had to obey. The voice of Shiwan Khan.

That voice had filled his mind ever since the night before. Lane had been looking out his lab window. Across the street was a huge billboard advertising cigarettes. It featured a happy smoker puffing out huge smoke rings.

"Silly fellow," Lane was thinking. "Smoking has to be bad for you. I'm sure that soon science will find out just how bad and then—"

That was as far as he got. At that moment, the smoker's face changed. Lane got his first look at Shiwan Khan. And heard his voice for the first time. Lane had no choice but to obey it. He had not stopped since.

Five Mongol warriors stood around the lab, waiting for Dr. Lane. They had come to take him to Shiwan Khan.

Suddenly the warriors heard a noise from the

lab balcony. They raised their crossbows to the ready. One went out onto the balcony to investigate.

Too late the warrior saw the black-gloved fist. It lashed him on the chin.

His crossbow went flying. But he was a Mongol warrior, trained to be as hard as nails.

He reached up and grabbed the gloved hand. He started wrestling with the black-cloaked figure. They teetered on the balcony edge. Unless one gave up, they were going to fall.

The Shadow didn't give up. He merely gave a half-turn in the air as they fell together.

That half-turn was enough to put the Mongol underneath him. The Mongol acted like a pillow when they hit a cement balcony two flights below.

The Shadow stood up. He looked down at the Mongol. The warrior was out cold.

"One down," The Shadow said. "Four to go."

A minute later, a second Mongol met The Shadow. His head snapped back and he sailed across the room. He lay stunned, wondering what had hit him.

This time no fist could be seen. The Shadow's terrifying laugh filled the room.

But the other three Mongols showed no fear. They waded in, throwing punches.

All they hit was empty air—air echoing with that mocking laugh.

Suddenly the laughing stopped—and the lights went out.

The second Mongol shook his battered head to clear it. Thinking fast, he grabbed a flashlight off a table and played the beam around the room. In moments he found what he was looking for.

Caught in the beam was a shadow on a wall. The shadow of a man in a cloak and a slouch hat.

The shadow darted right and left, but the light beam followed it. The other warriors quickly fired at the shadow. One of the crossbow arrows nicked it.

The flashlight beam showed a scrap of black cloth pinned to the wall. The Mongols whooped a battle cry. They nocked more arrows in their bows.

A second one found its mark.

The Mongols could see all of their enemy now. The man in a black cloak and slouch hat stood by the wall. He was pinned there by arrows through his cloak above both shoulders.

The Mongols grinned at each other. They

nocked more arrows. It was time for the kill.

But not the way they expected it.

They hadn't noticed one thing. The Shadow's hands were free.

Those hands went under his black cloak. They came out holding silver .45 automatics.

By the time the pistols emptied, two Mongols lay on the floor.

The Shadow didn't even glance at them.

All he saw was the lab door closing. A Mongol had escaped with Dr. Lane. The Shadow started after them—and was blindsided by the last Mongol.

The fight was over fast. The Shadow stood on the balcony, looking down. He hoped the falling Mongol hadn't hit Moe's cab. Moe took such pride in it.

The Shadow was grim. All he could do now was have Moe drive him home. He'd won the fight but lost precious time. Lane's trail was cold. There was no stopping Khan from making the scientist his slave. A slave that would help make Khan master of the world.

The only way to find and free Lane was to find and defeat Khan.

Unless, of course, Khan came looking for him.

▲
The Tulku awaits
the arrival of
Lamont Cranston.

◄
The voice of The
Shadow interrupts
mobsters about
to throw Dr. Roy
Tam over the
bridge.

◀
Dr. Roy Tam fears
for his life as The
Shadow approaches.

Lamont Cranston
discusses strategy
with right-hand man
Moe Shrevnitz.
▼

▲
Cranston obtains
information from
his uncle, Police
Commissioner
Wainright Barth.

Margo Lane
makes a dazzling
appearance at
the Cobalt Club.
▶

▲
Cranston and
Margo Lane say
good night.

A museum
guard struggles
to close the
latches on
Genghis Khan's
silver coffin.
▶

▲
Shiwan Khan, last descendant of Genghis Khan,
plots to conquer the world.

Dr. Reinhardt Lane, hard at work on Khan's atomic bomb.

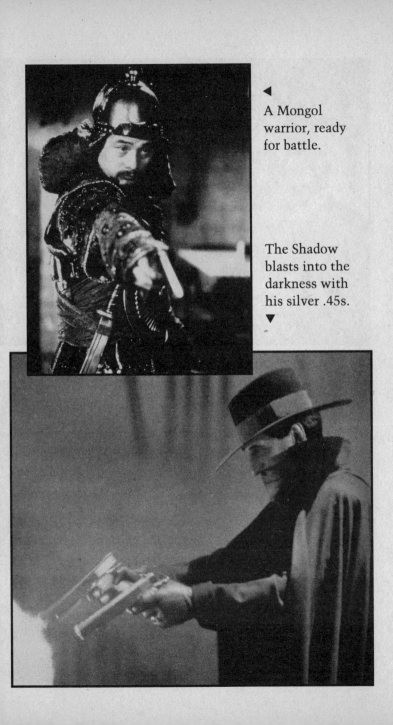

◄
A Mongol
warrior, ready
for battle.

The Shadow
blasts into the
darkness with
his silver .45s.
▼

▼ Farley Claymore floods his lab to trap The Shadow.

► Margo Lane rushes to The Shadow's aid.

◄ Cranston threatens Khan with the Tulku's ancient dagger.

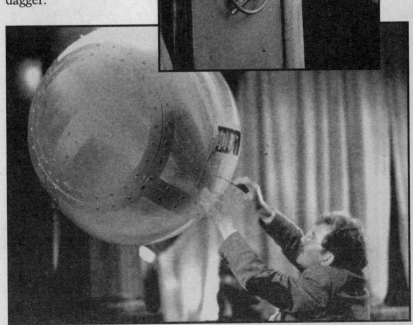

▲ Dr. Lane attempts to defuse the atomic bomb as precious seconds tick away.

▲
Lamont Cranston and Margo Lane enjoy a well-earned
night on the town.

Chapter 10

Lamont Cranston was in his bedroom when he heard the sound. Only ears as keen as a cat's could have picked it up. The front door of his mansion was being gently opened. He heard feet softly coming up the carpeted stairs. Then his bedroom door knob turning.

He knew what the sounds added up to. These were the sounds of a hunter.

The bedroom door opened. Cranston saw who the hunter was.

Margo Lane. With a long pistol in her hand.

She saw Cranston as well. She saw him sitting up in bed, facing her.

He was a hunter's dream—a perfect target.

Margo did not hesitate. She raised the pistol and fired. The bullet hit Cranston in the heart.

And he shattered into a thousand pieces.

Cranston looked at the shattered mirror behind

his bed. He was sitting in a chair across from it.

Now Margo stood frozen, seeing nothing.

Cranston knew who had the power to put Margo in a trance. But he needed details.

Cranston took the pistol out of Margo's hand. It was a beautifully made single-shot model. He didn't bother looking for the bullet that smashed the mirror. It was sure to be silver. Bronzium, in fact. Just like the coin Khan had left behind.

He put the pistol in a drawer. Then he put his lips near Margo's ear.

"Margo Lane," he said.

Her name brought her back to herself. She turned, dazed.

"Cranston," she said. "What are you doing here?"

"That should be my question," Cranston answered. "You're in my home. *Who sent you?*"

"I don't know," Margo said, bewildered. "There was this voice—this voice in my head. It was giving me orders—orders I had to obey."

"Where did you first hear this voice?" Cranston demanded.

"I got a call from Dad," Margo said. "He told me to go to his lab. When I got there, it was empty. But something made me look out the window. I saw a cigarette billboard ad. The face of a man blowing smoke rings. The face changed. Then everything went black. I don't remember how I got this pistol. I just remember the voice in my head."

"And the voice said?" Cranston asked.

"It said I had to kill—The Shadow." Margo paused. She looked hard at Cranston. "And I came *here*."

There was a silence as she continued to stare at Cranston.

It was broken by Cranston's harsh command, "Get out of here! Go! Now!"

But Margo only came closer. "Let me see into your eyes," she said.

"You won't like what you see," Cranston warned, backing away.

Margo refused to look away. "I always felt there was something strange about you," she said. "I could feel it. That static in my head, whenever I was near you."

"Watch what you say," Cranston said. "You're in *danger*."

Margo took another step toward him. *"You're The Shadow,"* she said.

With a low growl, Cranston grabbed Margo by

the arms. But he would not look into her eyes.

Margo didn't wince. Her voice was steady as a rock. "My father has disappeared. The police are useless. Only The Shadow can help me find him. What's your answer?"

Cranston fought to hold back the fury inside him. No one who came too close to his secret self was safe from it. And no one had ever come as close as Margo Lane.

He had to get out of there. He had to get away from her.

"Make sure you're gone when I get back," he said, heading for the door.

"You haven't answered me," Margo called after him. He didn't stop. She flung out a threat. "How do you know I won't tell the world who you really are?"

Cranston wheeled around. He came back to her. He let her look into his eyes. He let her see what might be in store for her.

"I know," he said.

He left then. She didn't follow him.

Someone else did.

Cranston sensed it as he waited outside for Moe Shrevnitz's cab. Something made him look up. Across the street he saw a parked car. The driver sat behind the wheel. He was a Mongol.

Moe's cab arrived.

"The Sanctum," Cranston commanded.

As Moe drove, Cranston looked in the rearview mirror. The Mongol's car kept right behind them.

Moe dropped Cranston off at Times Square. The man was still behind him.

This has gone far enough, Cranston thought. It was time to turn things around. The joke was going to be on Khan.

Cranston went into the alley leading to the Sanctum entrance. The Mongol followed. He peered into the darkness. He saw nothing.

The Shadow had to strain not to laugh at the look on the Mongol's face. Finally the Mongol turned away. The Shadow went after him.

He was no longer the hunted. He was the hunter.

He sat in the backseat of the Mongol's car on a drive down to Chinatown.

It was Lamont Cranston who got out of the car to follow him further. The twisting streets were crowded. It was too much trouble to cloud that many minds. Besides, there was no point. The Mongol Cranston followed was leading him to Shiwan Khan, and his mind could not be clouded.

Cranston trailed the Mongol up the narrow stairs of a second-floor restaurant. Cranston brushed aside the curtains at the entrance. The Mongol had vanished. There was just one person in the small dining room.

"Nice tie," Cranston told Shiwan Khan. "Nice suit, too. Brooks Brothers has good stuff."

"Thank you," Shiwan Khan said. He was picking meat off a bone with a large dagger. "Sit down and dig in. I've already ordered for you."

Cranston stayed standing. "Sure. You were expecting me. After you sent Margo Lane to kill me."

Shiwan Khan paused, the dagger halfway to his mouth. His face creased in a smile. "Kill you? If I wanted you dead, Ying Ko, you'd be chopped liver now. I sent the girl to *be* killed. Tell me, how did you do it?"

"She's alive," Cranston said.

Khan kept smiling. "For how long? She knows who you are. She's a danger to you. How long before your true self takes over?"

Cranston planted both hands on the table. He leaned forward, looking down at Khan.

"I know your plan, Khan," he said. "But you still don't have a beryllium sphere. Without it, you can't complete the bomb. You know I'll stop you first."

Khan scoffed. "You Americans are so confident," he replied. "You think your childish country is the new cradle of civilization. It will be a graveyard by the time I'm finished with it."

"Watch it, pal," Cranston said. "That's the U.S. of A. you're talking about."

Khan's voice boomed, "I'm talking about *ruling the world*!"

It was Cranston's turn to smile. "Take down this name. Leonard Levinsky. A brilliant psychiatrist. Your head needs a good shrink."

"You're *boring* me!" Khan said—and thrust his dagger down at Cranston's hand on the table.

Cranston didn't blink. He merely spread his fingers. The dagger hit the space between them.

"Good reflexes," said Khan approvingly.

Cranston wasn't listening. He was staring at the blade quivering in the tabletop. Staring back was a face carved in its handle.

"That dagger—" he said in a choked voice.

"Recognize it?" Khan said. "I took it from the Tulku. Or rather, I took it *out* of the Tulku. After I killed him with it."

With a gasp of rage, Cranston grabbed the dagger. He yanked it out of the table. He raised it to plunge into Khan's heart—if he had one.

Cranston gave a sob of pain. The face on the handle had come alive as it had many years before. Its teeth tore at his wrist.

The knife dropped from his hand—and slid to Khan's waiting hand, handle first.

"You still haven't learned," Khan said. "You can't master it with your will. You need a greater force. You must reach much further down within you. You have to give in to your instincts."

"Instincts," Cranston said. "I'll show you my instincts."

His hands went around Khan's throat. He heard Khan gurgle as he squeezed.

Suddenly, his hot rage chilled. Cold steel was pressing on his temple.

It was the long barrel of a single-shot pistol. The Mongol warrior was holding it to Cranston's head. In his other hand, the Mongol held a second single-shot pistol.

Cranston had no choice. He released Khan.

Khan rubbed his throat. "My Mongol warriors aren't very bright. But they are loyal."

The Mongol slowly stepped back, but he kept both guns trained on Cranston.

"Accept the truth," Khan urged. "You and I are part of the same dark shadow. Killing you would be like killing a twin brother. That's why you're here. I want to give you a last chance. Because I will have to kill you unless you give me the answer I crave. *Will you join me?*"

Chapter 11

Shiwan Khan stared hard at Cranston. "You cannot defeat me," Khan said. "You cannot fool me. Your mind is an open book."

Cranston did not return his stare. Cranston was looking in another direction—into the eyes of the Mongol warrior.

"Then learn how to read, Khan," Cranston said, and leapt up from the table.

The warrior looked pained as he raised his pistols—and tossed one of them to Cranston.

Khan moved fast. He sent the table flying toward Cranston. Jumping over to avoid it, Cranston couldn't get off his shot.

Khan dashed to the dazed warrior. He grabbed the other gun from the man's limp hand.

"Weakling," he snarled, and punched the warrior in the stomach. As the warrior collapsed, Khan turned toward Cranston. "Time for a duel,

Ying Ko. Let the stronger mind win."

He raised his pistol. Across the room, Cranston did the same.

Their two shots sounded like one.

Both their mouths dropped open in surprise.

The bullets had met in midair. They dropped to the floor fused into a single lump of metal.

Khan recovered first. "Thanks for the fun," he said. "We'll have to do it again. But right now I have to run."

He stared at the window. The glass exploded. Khan threw himself through the empty space.

Cranston pressed the red stone on his ring as he raced to the window. He looked out. Khan had landed on his feet. Waiting down the street was a motorcycle with a sidecar. A Mongol warrior sat in the driver's seat.

Cranston was running down the stairs as Moe's cab screeched to a stop at the curb.

"You found me. Good work," Cranston said, getting into the back.

"I been reading this book," Moe said. "How to develop your mental power."

"Good. See if you can use it to catch up with that motorcycle," said Cranston. "The one that just vanished around the corner."

"*That* I use my horsepower for," Moe said. His cab roared into motion.

Cranston had never seen anyone go faster on the city streets than Moe Shrevnitz. Not even a Mongol on a motorcycle who didn't know the meaning of fear.

Moe kept the cycle in sight as he wove through traffic and careened around corners. Then his eyes widened—and his foot pressed the brake.

The motorcycle was heading straight for a bridge pillar dividing the road.

The cab stopped. Moe watched the cycle and sidecar split apart just before the pillar. They went around the pillar on opposite sides. Then they hooked up again and were lost in the night.

Moe scratched his head. "I guess I didn't read that book far enough."

He started up the cab again. But there was no way of picking up the trail.

Suddenly Cranston said, "Stop here, Moe."

"Sure, boss," Moe said. "But there's nothing here. Just an empty lot. Looks like a building was torn down. And nobody had the dough to replace it. Happens a lot. Times are tough."

Cranston looked through a chain-link fence at the vacant lot. All he could see was rubble and weeds. Moe was probably right. Maybe the strange vibes that Cranston picked up came from ghosts of the past. Echoes of things dead and gone. The city was full of them.

"Where now, boss?" Moe asked.

There was only one place to go. The last place in the world Cranston wanted to go.

"Home," Cranston said, bracing himself for what he feared was waiting for him there.

She was.

Margo Lane was asleep on a sofa in the Cranston mansion. She woke as he came in.

"Don't send me away," she said. "I can help you find my father. You know that I have certain—powers. I never knew I had them before. But you bring them out in me."

"I just know what *you* bring out in *me*," Cranston said. "I'm afraid of what I might do to you. You should be, too."

Margo looked at him and smiled. "What's there to be afraid of?"

"You have no idea what I'm capable of," Cranston said. He walked over to the fireplace and stared into the heart of the licking flames. "I was just thirteen when I first found out. A cousin of mine tattled on me for cheating in school.

After school, I caught up with him."

Cranston looked down at his hands. They were clenching and unclenching uncontrollably. "My hands went around his throat. I saw his face turning color. I had never felt such power. It was a power greater than anything else inside of me. I still do not know how I stopped myself from finishing him off. I never was able to overcome that terrible power again. It is more than part of me. It *is* me. And there is no way I can keep myself from destroying anyone who threatens it—even someone I love."

He turned toward Margo—but she did not shrink from his burning gaze.

Her eyes met his. "Lamont, I'm not worried," she said. "I think I know you better than you know yourself."

Cranston glared at her. "You're leaving here— and that's that."

"We'll see—in the morning," Margo said. "I'll sleep on it. Pleasant dreams."

That night, though, Cranston's dreams were anything but pleasant.

The next morning Cranston woke unusually early. When he went to her room to wake her,

Cranston told Margo about one of his dreams.

"I dreamed I was in a room with you," he said. "You were sleeping like a baby. I moved toward you. On the way, I glimpsed my face in a mirror. There was a smudge on my cheek. I tried to rub it off—*and my skin started to peel away like a mask.*"

"Ugh," Margo grimaced.

"The face peeled all the way off," Cranston said. "Below was another face. A grinning face. *The face of Shiwan Khan.*"

"Shiwan Khan?" said Margo. "Who's he? Should I know him?"

Cranston didn't answer. He went on, "I picked up a knife. I raised it over you. That's when I woke up."

Margo put her hand on his shoulder. "Lamont, you have problems."

Cranston gaped at her in amazement.

Laughing, she said, "Relax, it was just a dream. I know a guy you should talk to. Dr. Leonard Levinsky. He'll tell you what it means."

"I know what it means," Cranston said. "And I know dreams can come true. Margo, it's time for you to leave. I've got a—"

"Taxi waiting?" Margo finished his sentence.

"What?" Cranston said, taken aback.

"Wasn't that what you were about to say?" Margo asked.

"Yes," Cranston said, between clenched teeth.

"The more I'm around you, the easier it gets," Margo said. "Knowing your thoughts is like reading a book. Anyway, I don't need a taxi."

"Yes, you do. I have to—" Cranston began.

"Good," Margo said. "I'll go with you."

"Let me finish a sentence for a change," Cranston snapped. He was getting sick of this open-book stuff. First Khan, now Margo. Pretty soon, he'd be out in paperback. "Last night we agreed that—"

"*You* agreed I was going to leave," Margo said. "I didn't agree to anything. We'll be a great team. Look how smoothly we mesh."

Cranston opened his mouth to answer. But before he could say a word, Margo cut in, "Yes we do. And no more arguments. Even if you don't need me, I need you—to find my father. No way you're going to shake me. I'm too close to you."

By now Cranston knew better than to waste his breath. "Okay."

"Now, where do we start?" Margo asked.

Cranston sighed, "You tell me."

Chapter 12

Moe dropped Cranston and Margo off at Times Square. But Cranston steered Margo away from the Sanctum. It was bad enough she could invade his mind. A man had to have some privacy.

As they walked, he told her about the terrifying power of the bomb.

"Hard to believe Dad would make something like *that*," Margo said.

"Scientists don't always know where their research will lead," Cranston said. "They're like slaves to their work. And now your father is a different kind of slave. A slave to Shiwan Khan."

Margo looked at the tall buildings around them, shutting off the sky. "I can't imagine that a single bomb could destroy all this."

"Manhattan is perfect place to set it off," Cranston said grimly. "A tiny island jammed with skyscrapers and packed with people. I can see

Khan looking at it and laughing with glee."

Margo shuddered.

"Don't worry," Cranston said. "Khan still needs one more thing to make it work. A beryllium sphere. If we can find out where he intends to get one—"

Margo stopped dead in her tracks.

"A beryllium sphere?" she said.

"Right," Cranston said. "Now as I was saying—"

"Farley Claymore!" she exclaimed.

"What? Who?" Cranston asked.

"My dad's assistant," Margo said. "A creep. He wants to date me. Ugh. He tries to impress me by boasting about his work. He's working on a beryllium sphere. I'm sure of it."

"In your father's lab?" asked Cranston. His voice was tense.

"No, he's working on his own," said Margo. "The Mari-Tech labs, way downtown. Shall we go see him?"

"I've got another job for you," Cranston told her.

"What?" Margo asked, eager to help.

"Last night I was trailing Khan," Cranston said.

"I lost him at the corner of Houston Street and Second Avenue. There's just an empty lot there—but there's something funny about it. I want you to go to City Hall. Find out what used to be there."

"Sure. Easy," Margo said. "But what about Farley Claymore?"

"Ever been to his lab?" Cranston asked.

Margo grimaced. "Once," she said. "The creep lured me down there to show off his sphere."

"What's the lab's layout?" Cranston asked.

"It's in a weird metal building," Margo said. "It's round, has just one door, and no windows. It looks like a big soup can. The lab is on the second floor. The only way in is through a raised hatchway in the floor. It's like going into a submarine."

"Thanks, Margo," Cranston said. "I have to apologize. You are a help. Anything else you can think of about the lab?"

Margo thought a second. "There are all kinds of pipes leading into it. Seems Claymore needs a lot of water for his work—the drip. But why all the questions?"

Cranston smiled. "Mr. Farley Claymore is going to get a little visit."

Farley Claymore's lab was exactly as Margo described it. So was Farley Claymore.

He was as simpleminded a scientist as ever cheated his way to a degree. But he had stumbled onto the secret of making a beryllium sphere. Even in science there was such a thing as dumb luck.

Today, however, Farley Claymore had a feeling that his luck had run out.

He heard a deep voice demanding, "Where is the beryllium sphere, Claymore?"

Claymore looked frantically around his lab. Its curving walls were smooth and seamless. The hatch leading to it was closed. There wasn't even a place for a roach to hide. But he saw no one.

"Sphere?" he said weakly. "What sphere?"

The voice boomed out. "Claymore, you idiot! Your mind is being controlled by a force of evil."

"My mind—controlled?" said Claymore.

The voice replied, "The sphere, Claymore! What have you done with it?"

"It's too late," Claymore said, shaking his head dully. "I loaded it onto a truck."

"Take me to that truck!" the voice of The Shadow commanded. *"Do it now!"*

"Never!" screamed Claymore.

He dropped his dazed act. He raced like a madman to a lever on a control panel. He pulled it. Water started seeping up through the floor ducts.

"No one controls my mind, Shadow," he shouted. "You see, I know who you are. Khan told me. And I tell you, I gladly work for Khan! There's a new world order coming! And I'm going to be a king! You hear me! A king!"

His eyes gleamed insanely as he whipped out a gun and looked around wildly.

"Who do you think you're going to shoot with that?" The Shadow mocked.

But Claymore's eyes had stopped darting. They were fixed at one spot on the floor. The water seeping into the room was swirling around two obstacles. Two invisible obstacles. Two invisible legs.

Claymore aimed his gun in that direction—and pulled the trigger six times.

The echoes of the shots died away. Claymore went to the wall where the bullets had hit. They left evenly spaced holes. But there was a gap in the row. One bullet had not made it to the wall. It had hit something else.

Claymore saw blood dripping into the water.

He shrieked with laughter. He threw another switch on his control panel. Water gushed into the room.

"I'll be gone for a while, Shadow," he shouted. "I might be back—but don't hold your breath!"

In a blink, he was down through the hatchway, still a few inches above the rising water. He shut it tight above him. Airtight. And locked from the outside.

Inside the lab, the Shadow staggered to his feet. He clutched his bleeding shoulder. He felt the water rising to his waist. He looked for a way out. There was no exit.

"Margo," he said. "I need you."

But his voice was weak.

Margo was so far away.

And death was so near.

Chapter 13

The water rose higher with every desperate breath Cranston took. Soon there were just four inches of air between the water and the ceiling. Then two inches. Then none.

Cranston took one last desperate gulp of air, then swam underwater from wall to wall, looking for a way out. His lungs were bursting. Soon he would black out. Then he would relax. The pain in his lungs would go away. Everything would go away. Death was coming closer with every heart-beat. And it was looking more and more inviting.

"Got to keep fighting. Can't give in," he told himself. His eyes roamed the curving metal walls. He saw a row of holes—the bullet holes. Water was going through them. Not enough to drain the water gushing into the room. But enough to tell Cranston that the bullets had pierced the walls.

He swam to the holes with the last of his

strength. He stuck his finger into one, blocking it. Then he yanked the finger back out. Before water could pour into the hole again, he pressed his mouth to it. He blew the stale air out of his lungs. Then he sucked—hard. He tasted fresh air. He had never tasted anything so good.

He kept his mouth pressed against the hole. He breathed in and out through it. The bullets meant to kill him had saved him—for the moment. He had cheated death. But it would still win in the end, when his strength ran out.

Suddenly he felt a sucking force at his feet. It was pulling him downward. He was yanked away from his breathing hole. He groaned to himself. He had lost his last chance.

But he soon saw he was wrong.

The hatchway in the floor had been opened. Water was pouring out through it.

His head bobbed above water as its level dropped. Then his feet hit the floor. His legs half-buckled as he stood dripping and groggy. But he straightened up in surprise as he saw who came up through the hatchway.

"You called?" asked Margo.

"You heard?" gasped Cranston. Then he collapsed to the floor and fainted dead away.

When he came to, he was home in bed. Margo was looking at him.

When she saw his eyes open, she smiled in relief.

"I was in City Hall when I heard you," she said. "I didn't know where you were. I had to let my mind go blank. I had to trust I would go to the right place."

Cranston shook his head. "Margo, you scare me more and more. You know so much. You see so much."

"I have to confess, I saw a lot while you were sleeping," Margo said. She looked a little guilty. "I didn't mean to. But you were sleeping with your eyes open. I looked into them."

"What did you see?" Cranston asked sharply.

"I saw someone who was you, yet who *wasn't* you," Margo said, puzzled. "He was dressed like an Asian lord. He was on a battlefield. He was unbelievably savage. Unbelievably cruel."

"I'm afraid you'd better believe it," Cranston said sadly. "I've done things I can never forgive myself for. Things I couldn't stop myself from doing. Things I didn't want to stop myself from doing. Things I *burned* to do."

"But that was all in the past," Margo said.

"That part of your life is over now."

"No, Margo," Cranston said. "It will never be over for me."

"I refuse to believe you," Margo insisted.

"Then believe someone who knows," Cranston told her. He smiled grimly. "The Shadow knows."

A wave of weariness washed over him.

Margo saw it. "Try to rest," she said. "You're still weak."

"I want to find out what—" Cranston began.

"I'll tell you what I found out at City Hall later," Margo assured him. "Just take a little nap now."

"Still reading my mind," said Cranston. "Promise me one thing—"

"I promise," Margo said. "If you have any more dreams, I won't peek."

Cranston had no dreams this time. Falling asleep was like falling into a deep black hole. He had no idea how long he slept. Or how much longer he would have slept—if Margo hadn't woken him.

"I'm sorry," she said. "But I knew you'd want to see this."

She thrust a newspaper into his hands.

The headline read: MADMAN THREATENS TO BLOW

Margo filled him in on the details. "Khan demands more than money. He wants the finest art, the most precious jewels. He wants it all by midnight tonight—the Chinese New Year. But the government doesn't believe him. They don't think his bomb exists. They've refused to pay."

She looked at Cranston imploringly. "You don't really think that Khan will—"

"New York is dead—unless we find Khan's hideout," Cranston said. "Quick, tell me. What did you find out about that vacant lot?"

"Not much, " Margo said. "The Hotel Monolith was the last building on it. The place was finished ten years ago. But it never opened. The builder went bust. Somebody from the Far East bought it. And that was the last of it."

"When was it torn down?" asked Cranston.

"Funny about that," Margo said. "I checked the city records. Then I went through old newspapers and made a lot of phone calls. Everybody knew it had been torn down. But nobody knew when or why."

"Or *if*," Cranston said.

"What do you mean?" Margo asked.

"I mean," Cranston said, "we need to get down

to that vacant lot. And we need to do it fast."

Moe sped them downtown. But when they arrived, the cabbie scratched his head. "I don't see what all the hurry was about, boss. This is one place where nothing is happening. Just maybe the weeds grew a little."

While Moe waited in the cab, Cranston and Margo got out to take a better look.

"I have to agree with Moe," Margo said. She saw only rubble and weeds. The scene was bleak under dark clouds that covered the sky.

Cranston paid no attention to her. All his attention was focused on the vacant lot.

"I can't believe he did it," Cranston muttered. His forehead creased. Sweat beaded his brow as he strained to *see*.

"Did what?" Margo asked. For once Cranston had left her far behind.

She could only scan his sweating face for clues. She saw it suddenly brighten.

"It's beautiful," he gasped. Before his eyes stood a magnificent luxury hotel. It was fit for a king. Or for a Khan.

"Khan hypnotized the whole city. Nobody sees it," Cranston said. But he wasn't talking to Margo. He was talking to himself. Margo was forgotten.

Everything was forgotten except the excitement boiling up in him. "But *I* see."

"What?" Margo said. "The hotel? Lamont, *tell* me."

Cranston's voice was cold. "You and Moe will receive instructions. Follow them exactly."

"Lamont," said Margo, "if you know where Khan is, we can get help!"

Cranston didn't answer. He didn't even look at Margo. He went to the cab. He took a parcel from the backseat. Then he walked swiftly away.

Margo had to half-run to keep up with him. "Lamont, you don't have to do this yourself!" she pleaded.

He headed down an alley. Still she followed him.

He stopped. She did, too, a few feet away.

The black slouch hat went on his head. Its shadow fell over his face.

"Lamont, this isn't who you really are!" Margo cried. She came closer to his shadowed face. She wanted to see what was in his burning eyes.

Boom! A deafening thunderclap came from the clouds. Blinding lightning forked down.

Margo blinked her eyes to clear them. But what she saw made her want to shut them again.

A nightmare figure stood in a black cloak flapping madly in the lashing wind.

"*This* is who I am," The Shadow said.

And his laugh raged around her like the breaking storm.

Chapter 14

First Shiwan Khan had made the Hotel Monolith invisible to outsiders. Then he had turned it into his dream house.

Now he sat in his favorite room. The throne room. Flanking him were Mongol warriors. In front of him stood Dr. Reinhardt Lane and Farley Claymore.

Dr. Lane stood with empty eyes and a dim-witted smile. Claymore's eyes gleamed in triumph. His smile was like a shark's.

Beside them was Claymore's beryllium sphere. Inside it was the bomb that Dr. Lane had just finished making.

Khan came down from his throne. He went to Claymore.

"You are my special servant," he said. "The only American to join me of his own free will."

"It was my pleasure," Claymore said, trying to look modest.

Khan put his hand tenderly on Claymore's cheek. "And you wanted so little in return," Khan said. He put his other hand on the other cheek. "Just to be a king."

Khan began to squeeze.

"King? I said that? *Bad* choice of words," Claymore gasped out. "I meant prince, tops. Or duke? Baron? Your choice. Whatever you say."

Khan let him go.

"A warning, my loyal servant," Khan said.

"Right," Claymore said, rubbing his cheek.

"Now activate the bomb," Khan ordered.

"Yes sir, yes sir," Claymore said. He turned to Dr. Lane. "Thought I was just a simple tool, huh? You never figured I'd become the right-hand man of a conqueror."

"Not you," Khan said. "I was talking to Dr. Lane. Lane, do it!"

Lane's dopey smile stayed on his face as he hit a switch. In the bomb's glass face, cards started flipping. The first one read two hours, no minutes, and no seconds. The next one, a second less. The countdown had begun.

Khan gazed at it gleefully. Then he said to

Claymore. "You're sure you can duplicate this bomb whenever I want one?"

"Piece of cake," Claymore assured him.

"Then I don't need Dr. Lane." He turned to a guard. "Take Lane to the next room. Tie him up. His own invention will kill him."

Claymore coughed. "Look, I don't want to be pushy. But don't *we* have to clear out of here?"

"You think I don't think of everything?" Khan demanded.

"Yes sir," Claymore said. "I mean, no sir. I mean—"

Khan cut him off with a wave of his hand. "There is an airplane waiting to fly us to safety. We leave in one hour."

Suddenly Khan stiffened. "What was that?" he hissed.

"Must be thunder," Claymore said. "It's really storming outside."

"That was no thunder, you fool," Khan said. "It was the front doors downstairs banging open."

"But nobody can see this place," Claymore said. "And you have all those guards down there."

"One man could see my castle. One man could get by my guards," Khan said. *"Ying Ko."*

"The Shadow," gulped Claymore.

"Find him and kill him," Khan commanded.

"Kill *him*? *Me*?" Claymore said.

"All of you!" Khan said.

"I'd rather stay and help you," Claymore offered.

"Go!" Khan ordered, and handed Claymore a Tommy gun.

"But—" Claymore said. That was as far as he got. Three guards grabbed him and hustled him off.

"I hope you guys know what you're doing," Claymore said as they moved through the corridors.

One of the guards smiled. He pulled out a flashlight. He'd caught The Shadow in its beam once before, in Lane's lab. He'd do it again here.

"*Heh-heh-heh-heh.*" The Shadow's laugh came from the end of the hallway.

Claymore tore the flashlight from the Mongol's hand. He jerked his head in the direction of the laugh.

"You guys go that way," he said—and took off in the opposite direction.

Behind him he heard shots. "Those bozos will keep The Shadow busy," he muttered. "I'll have some breathing room to find a place to hide."

He ran through a doorway. He was in a ball-room. There was no place to hide on its bare floor. On the other side of the room was an open door. He ran for it.

It slammed in his face. Then the door behind him slammed shut.

Frantically Claymore played his flashlight around the vast room. His finger was tense on the Tommy gun trigger.

"Did you actually think you'd seen the last of me?" The Shadow's voice thundered.

"I'll see you, all right," screamed Claymore. "I'll see you dead!"

A shadow appeared in his flashlight beam. The shadow of a man in a cloak and slouch hat.

Shaking with silent laughter, Claymore blasted it.

"*Heh-heh-heh-heh.*" The Shadow's laugh echoed through the room.

Another shadow appeared on another wall, and Claymore blasted away again.

"I'm right here—all around you," The Shadow mocked, as another shadow appeared. And another. And another. And another. Until every wall was lined with shadows. And the smoking Tommy gun was empty.

Claymore dropped his gun and fell to his knees.

The Shadow gave another laugh.

"Coward! Chicken!" Claymore screamed. "Come out and fight like a man!"

Someone cleared his throat behind him.

The man in the slouch hat and black cloak stood looking down at him. The Shadow reached down and lifted Claymore up. He pulled him close, face to face.

Claymore's eyes bulged like a frog's. They seemed set to pop out of their sockets. In an instant, the strings of his mind snapped.

"Claymore, you're…you're…" The Shadow grimaced. "You're drooling, Claymore."

He dropped Claymore to the floor. Claymore lay there in a shuddering, slobbering heap.

The Shadow move on, heading for his next target. There was no time to waste.

The bomb was ticking.

Shiwan Khan was waiting.

It was showdown time.

Chapter 15

Outside the hotel, Moe Shrevnitz and Margo Lane stood under umbrellas in the pouring rain.

"Know what I like about this job?" Moe cracked. "The excitement." He scratched his head. "Any idea why we're standing here, staring at a vacant lot?"

"We have to follow The Shadow's orders," Margo said. "The Shadow knows." She shivered. Despite her umbrella, the rain was getting to her. "At least I hope he does."

Inside the hotel, The Shadow knew what he had to do. Find Shiwan Khan.

That part was easy. He followed a golden corridor to a massive door. He pushed. The door swung open. There in the great throne room sat Shiwan Khan. Khan smiled as The Shadow charged in. He jokingly stuck his hands out to be handcuffed.

But The Shadow wasn't in a joking mood.

He almost tripped over his own feet as he headed for Khan. He was too eager, he told himself. He had to fight to regain his balance.

The Shadow whipped out his .45s from under his cloak. He blasted away at Khan. There was no way he could miss.

But he did. Every shot missed.

As his jaw dropped in shock, The Shadow felt himself losing his balance again. He had to brace his feet to keep from falling.

"Fool!" Khan shouted. "This room is built on an angle. You couldn't hit me in a million years."

The Shadow spied a dagger hanging in a sheath on the wall. He grabbed it. "I won't miss with *this*," he snarled.

He was answered by Khan's roar of laughter.

He looked down. He recognized the dagger. The dagger of the Tulku.

The face on the handle recognized him as well. The dagger came to life in his hand. He couldn't stop it from slashing at his legs and arms. The Shadow tightened his grip and struggled to point it at Khan again. But the dagger would not obey. It slammed him against one wall, then another. It ripped away his cloak and slouch hat.

The Shadow was stripped away. Now it was Lamont Cranston who lay bleeding on the floor. The knife was at his throat. With the last of his strength, Cranston tried to keep it from finishing him off. The dagger tip pricked his throat.

Khan's face creased in merriment. "You can't control yourself," he crowed. "How can you hope to master the sacred dagger?"

Khan was right. Brute force only bred a greater brute force in the dagger. But what if...

He had to know, even if it was the last thing he ever did.

Cranston stopped trying to make the dagger do his will. He let his hand fall open. He let the dagger have its way.

It quivered and made a half-turn on his open palm. In a flash, it sailed across the room and buried itself just below Khan's heart!

Khan screamed and fell to the floor, bleeding. With the blood went his power, fading fast.

Outside the hotel, Margo and Moe saw the hotel appear. It was like a ship coming out of the fog. Within moments, they could see it all. They gazed with awe at the magnificent building.

"Let's go," Moe said.

They had their orders. Moe hoisted a crowbar. He broke through the iron gate in the hotel fence.

Together they dashed for the front door.

They followed the trail The Shadow had left. A heap of Mongol warriors. Then the whimpering remains of Claymore. They didn't stop until they reached the throne room. They swung the massive door open.

No one was there. They saw only an empty throne. And a strange device that showed seconds ticking away.

Margo knew what it was. "The bomb," she said.

At that moment, a figure entered the room.

Margo's face lit with joy. "Dad!" she said.

Dr. Reinhardt Lane rubbed his forehead. "Where am I? I feel like I've been asleep for a year."

"I'll explain it all—later," Margo said. She looked at the bomb face. It showed fifty minutes left. "But first, you have to turn this thing off."

Dr. Lane looked at it. "A beautiful piece of work," he said approvingly. "Who made it?"

"Dad," Margo groaned. "You did."

"I did?" Dr. Lane asked. "And you say you want me to turn it off?"

Margo forced herself to speak very slowly. "That's right, Dad. *Turn it off.*"

Dr. Lane turned it around. He inspected the tangle of wires in the back. "Hmmm," he said. "What happens if I yank this one?"

"Dad!" Margo screamed, as the cards in front started flipping like mad. Forty, twenty, ten, five—

"Okay, it's not that one," Dr. Lane said. He replaced the wire.

The cards slowed to real time.

There were two minutes left.

"You're sure *I* made this?" Dr. Lane asked his daughter.

"Where are you, Shadow, now that we need you?" Margo moaned.

"Yeah, where is he?" Moe echoed.

Chapter 16

The Shadow was in a fight to the finish.

It began while Moe and Margo were still outside the mansion. In the throne room, Cranston and Shiwan Khan faced each other. Cranston was in bad shape. Khan was even worse off. But the dagger had missed his heart.

Khan grunted as he pulled the dagger out. Staggering, he ducked behind a rug hanging on the wall.

Cranston clicked fresh bullet clips into his .45s. Then he whipped aside the rug.

He stared at the silver coffin of Genghis Khan. It stood upright against the wall.

"Bad hiding place, Shiwan," Cranston said. "It'll be your coffin now."

Cranston opened the coffin.

It was empty.

"Should have known," Cranston muttered.

"Khan's too foxy to box himself in."

Cranston took a deep breath. He stepped into the coffin and closed the lid behind him.

As the lid clicked shut, a door opened in the back. Cranston nodded. A fox always has more than one way out of its den. Guns held ready, Cranston moved through the doorway.

It was pitch-black. But in the distance he could see a dim light. He headed for it.

Crack! His forehead smacked into something. Something hard. He fell to the ground, dazed.

"Ha-ha-ha-ha!" Khan's cackling laugh filled the darkness.

Shaking his head, Cranston lurched to his feet. He stuck out one of his pistols. The barrel tapped against a hard surface. He felt it with his palm. It was glass—a thick wall of clear glass. He felt along it until he reached its edge. Watching out for other traps, he went around it.

He moved cautiously, eyes fixed on the distant light. Suddenly he stopped. He squinted. Khan was standing in light, smiling at him.

It was a long shot. But Cranston didn't hesitate. Nor did he miss.

Bang! Cranston's aim was true. The .45 slug hit Khan right between the eyes.

But Khan didn't fall. His head didn't even move. Instead, it turned into a spiderweb.

Khan laughed as blazing light suddenly filled the room. Cranston ducked his head, momentarily blinded. When he looked up, he found himself surrounded. Shiwan Khan was everywhere.

Cranston was in a long hall of mirrors. His bullet had hit one. But there were hundreds more. Each one contained a laughing Khan, flashing a dagger. Cranston's eyes darted from one to another. It was no use. There was no way to tell which one was real.

Until he heard a sound behind him. Cranston whirled to see Khan's leering face. He jumped back as Khan lunged at him with the dagger. Before Cranston could even raise his .45s, Khan vanished again.

Cranston looked down at his shirt. It was torn right above his belt. He had pulled back just in time.

Cranston grimaced and started back down the hall. His trigger fingers were itching.

"Come no further, Ying Ko," Khan called to him. "This is the last place you want to be."

In response, Cranston began to move faster. He passed one reflection of Khan after another.

But the mirrors seemed to have no end.

"*This* is the place that tells the truth," Khan called. His voice was even more distant.

Cranston broke into a run. He'd catch up with Khan and then he'd—

Cranston froze as Khan's voice thundered, "*Ying Ko. Look into your past!*"

Khan was no longer in the mirrors. Cranston was.

Cranston, on horseback, slashing at helpless victims with his sword. Cranston, on his Tibetan throne, sentencing his closest friend to death. Cranston, as a schoolboy, his hands around his cousin's throat. Cranston, in his New York City mansion, grabbing Margo Lane by the arms.

"*No!*" Cranston screamed. His guns clattered to the floor. He covered his face with his hands.

"Yes!" Khan shouted.

Cranston parted his hands. Khan stood before him, dagger raised.

Cranston threw up his hands to block Khan's thrusts. He braced himself, but the thrusts didn't come. He looked up.

Again Khan was in all the mirrors, watching him. And laughing. Cranston sank to his knees.

Khan's laughter subsided to a chuckle. "Poor

Ying Ko," Khan said mockingly. "You could never decide who you are. Now *I* must decide for you. And I decide—*you will be nothing!*"

All the Khans raised their daggers for the death blow.

But Cranston wasn't listening. He wasn't looking.

A blue vein stood out on his forehead. Sweat beaded on his face. The pupils of his eyes were pinpricks. His eyeballs began to bulge.

The hall of mirrors began to rumble.

"What are you doing?" demanded Khan. "*Stop!*"

The rumbling in the hall turned into a grinding. One by one the mirrors exploded. They sounded like a string of firecrackers.

The last of the mirrors shattered. There was a sudden silence. Khan stood exposed before Cranston, his clothes soaked with the blood from his chest wound.

"Very impressive, Ying Ko," Khan said. "But destroying my mirrors will not stop your death."

Khan raised the dagger and moved toward Cranston.

But Cranston didn't look up. He was staring at a sharp piece of glass in front of him. Slowly, it began to rise into the air.

Khan stared at the glass, mesmerized.

"*No!*" he cried, as the glass suddenly descended toward his head. Khan froze, his eyes glazing over. Then he collapsed, his dagger clattering to the floor.

Cranston walked over to where Khan lay. Khan was unconscious, but still breathing.

"Tough luck, pal," Cranston said. "I guess nobody ever told you—bad guys finish last."

He threw Khan over his shoulders and looked at his watch. Still plenty of time before the bomb went off. He probably wouldn't even have to bother with it. Moe and Margo were on the job. Between them, they couldn't miss.

But Cranston was wrong. Very wrong.

At that moment, Moe and Margo were crouched over the bomb with Dr. Lane.

The cards were still flipping.

Chapter 17

Dr. Lane was the only scientist in the world who could have put the bomb together. And he was the only one who could take it apart.

"It's a work of genius," he said, studying it.

"Dad, I've already told you, *you* made it," Margo said.

Dr. Lane mused. "A fascinating case of memory loss. I'll have to do research on it. Maybe get a government grant."

"Some other time, Dad," Margo said. "Right now, just try to remember how this thing works."

Dr. Lane studied it. "It has a timing mechanism. Those flipping cards in front."

"We know that," Margo groaned.

"Do we ever," said Moe.

"Let's see," Dr. Lane went on. "They read one minute. Now fifty-nine seconds. Now—"

"Dad!" Margo said.

"Well, those wires only speeded them," Lane said. He indicated the first ones he had pulled. "Let's see about *these*."

He gave a yank.

"Ooops," he said, as clamps holding the bomb in place lifted away.

The bomb fell to the slanting floor and started to roll away from them. Faster and faster.

"Grab it!" Margo shouted.

It stayed ahead of their clutching hands. It rolled out the door. Panting, they chased it down the hallway. They lost ground with every step.

"Oh no," said Margo. The ball was heading for a gaping hole at the end of the hall. Unpaid workman must have left the floor unfinished.

"Good-bye," Moe said to their chances.

"Hel-*lo*," Margo said, racing ahead. The bomb was a half inch too big for the hole. It was stuck there. Nothing was broken, though. The cards were still flipping.

The three of them crouched over it.

"Ten seconds," Dr. Lane noted. "Nine—"

"Pick a wire," Margo demanded. "Any wire."

"Let's see," Dr. Lane said, looking at the maze of wires.

"Don't see," Margo said. *"Do."*

"Five seconds," Moe groaned.

"Well, it's usually a green one," said Dr. Lane, reaching for one.

Margo seized his wrist and pulled it back.

"Dad!" she said. "I've told you a million times. That's *red. This* is green."

She grabbed the green wire and yanked with all her might.

It came loose.

"One second," Moe said, as the last card began to flip.

Then it froze.

"Whew," Margo said, sagging with relief.

"Hmmm," Dr. Lane said. "That's red. This is green. I think I have it now."

At that moment, Lamont Cranston arrived. He was carrying Khan like a sack over one shoulder.

He glanced at the bomb.

"I see you managed to stop it," he said.

"Piece of cake," Margo said.

"I figured," said Cranston. "Well, let's clear out before the police get here."

Outside they found a throng of people ringing the hotel. Policemen forced their way through the crowd. Commissioner Barth was with them.

"Ah, Miss Lane," he said. "I see you found your

father. I told you there was nothing wrong."

"You were right as always, Commissioner," Margo said sweetly.

"But what are you doing here?" he asked.

"I heard about this building," she said. "I came to see it like everybody else."

"I bet The Shadow is behind it," Barth said. "It bears his weird stamp. The man's a maniac."

"He's no maniac," Margo flared. "He's—"

Cranston coughed behind Margo.

Moe caught her eye and gave her a hard stare.

"He's who?" Barth demanded.

"He's a myth," Margo said weakly.

"Definitely," Cranston seconded.

"I should have known you'd be here," Barth said to his nephew. "Nothing better to do. But who's that man you're holding?"

"A delivery man for a Chinese restaurant," Cranston explained. "Got hit by a cab I was in."

"Yeah," Moe said. "He ran right in front of us. I tried to brake—but the road was too wet."

"Still, I feel a bit responsible," Cranston said. "I'm taking him to a good doctor."

Cranston wasn't lying about that. He took Khan to a very good doctor. In fact, he took him to the best surgeon in the city.

He left Khan in the doctor's hands.

The doctor was taking his surgical gloves off when Khan came to. A ring with a red stone gleamed on the doctor's finger.

"What's going on? Where am I?" Khan asked groggily.

"Relax," the doctor told him.

Khan replied with a snarl and sat up in bed. Only then did he notice his arms were strapped to his sides. He swung his legs out of bed and staggered to his feet.

"Release me at once," he commanded.

"Let's just follow the doctor's orders," the doctor said soothingly.

"I'll show you how to follow orders," Khan roared. "Look into my eyes, slave."

"Sure," said the doctor. "Knock yourself out."

Khan stared even harder. Then he screamed, *"What have you done to me?"*

"Saved your life, that's what," the doctor said. "Of course, I did have to take a little chunk out of your brain. But you'll never miss it. It's a part nobody ever uses." The doctor chuckled. "Unless of course you believe in mind control."

"You idiot!" Khan shrieked. "Don't you realize who I am? The last descendant of Genghis

Khan! The rightful ruler of the world!"

"Of course you are," the doctor said.

The doctor pressed a buzzer. Two attendants came in with a straitjacket.

"What's this one?" the first attendant asked.

"The last descendant of Genghis Khan," the doctor told him.

"Another one?" the second griped. "That makes six. The others ain't gonna like it."

Khan stared at one of the attendants. "Obey me," he growled.

"Right," the attendant said. "Whatever you say, Mr. Khan. Now, if you'll just come with us—"

"I'll get you for this, Ying Ko!" Khan screamed as he was led out of the room.

But the man who had been Ying Ko was far out of earshot.

Lamont Cranston was walking down Broadway. He was taking Margo Lane to dinner.

"Somehow I don't feel like Chinese tonight," Cranston told her. "Let's try Italian."

Then he stopped. He looked down an alley. It was the one that led to the Sanctum.

Margo put her hand gently on his tense arm. "You'll never have to go down that alley again.

You don't have to be The Shadow anymore. You defeated the dark spirit within you. And you defeated Shiwan Khan. The world is safe from madmen who want to conquer the globe."

Cranston's mouth tightened. "Is it?"

"Of course," Margo said. "This is the twentieth century."

Cranston didn't say anything.

He was looking into the darkness—the darkness of what was to come.

He saw a face emerge from that darkness.

It was a face with a funny mustache. But there was nothing funny about its burning eyes. Those eyes could cloud the minds of millions—and kill many millions more.

The Shadow *knew*. He would have to return.

Again and again and again.

For as long as evil lurked in the hearts of men.